W9-BNQ-845

Introduction

When I was very young, I loved to have my mother read to me before I went to sleep. Each night we would take a book to my bed and turn the pages slowly as we shared the pictures, poems, and stories.

As I grew older and learned to read, I would gather my bears and dolls around my bed and read to them.

I am no longer a child and my bears and dolls are older too, but we still like to read, especially at night before we go to sleep.

Now that it is *your* bedtime, I would like to share some of my favorite poems and pictures with you. Then, when it is time for you to go to sleep, turn out the light and dream sweet dreams. . . . The bears will be waiting in your bedtime book for tomorrow night!

Michele Durkson Clise

A COLLECTION OF POEMS
TO READ AND SHARE

Selected by

Michele Durkson Clise

VIKING

For Jonathan Etra,
who always shared

VIKING
Published by the Penguin Group
Penguin Books USA Inc., 375 Hudson Street, New York, New York 10014, U.S.A.
Penguin Books Ltd, 27 Wrights Lane, London W8 5TZ, England
Penguin Books Australia Ltd, Ringwood, Victoria, Australia
Penguin Books Canada Ltd, 10 Alcorn Avenue, Toronto, Ontario, Canada M4V 3B2
Penguin Books (N.Z.) Ltd, 182-190 Wairau Road, Auckland 10, New Zealand

Penguin Books Ltd, Registered Offices: Harmondsworth, Middlesex, England

First published in 1994 by Viking, a division of Penguin Books USA Inc.

10 9 8 7 6 5 4 3 2 1

Grateful acknowledgment is made for permission to reprint the following copyrighted works:

"Bedtime" from *Eleanor Farjeon's Poems for Children*. Originally appeared in *Over the Garden Wall* by Eleanor Farjeon. Copyright 1933, renewed 1961 by Eleanor Farjeon. Reprinted by permission of HarperCollins Publishers.

"Sleeping Outdoors" from *Rhymes About Us* by Marchette Chute. Published 1974 by E. P. Dutton. Copyright 1974 by Marchette Chute. Reprinted by permission of Elizabeth Roach.

"The Night" from *Whispers and Other Poems* by Myra Cohn Livingston. © 1958 Myra Cohn Livingston. Copyright renewed 1986 Myra Cohn Livingston. Reprinted by permission of Marian Reiner for the author.

"Questions at Night" by Louis Untermeyer. By permission of the Estate of Louis Untermeyer, Norma Anchin Untermeyer % Professional Publishing Services.

"The Night Will Never Stay" by Eleanor Farjeon. Originally appeared in *Meeting Mary* by Eleanor Farjeon. Copyright © 1951, renewed 1979 by Gervase Farjeon. Reprinted by permission of HarperCollins Publishers.

Library of Congress Cataloging-in-Publication Data
Ophelia's bedtime book : a collection of poems to read and share / selected by Michele Durkson Clise. p. cm.
Summary: An illustrated collection of bedtime poems by such authors as Robert Louis Stevenson, Alfred, Lord Tennyson, and Eugene Field.
ISBN 0-670-85310-0
1. Sleep—Juvenile poetry. 2. Night—Juvenile poetry. 3. Children's poetry.
[1. Sleep—Poetry. 2. Night—Poetry. 3. Poetry—Collections.] I. Clise, Michele Durkson.
PN6110.S55064 1994 808.81'9353—dc20 93-41485 CIP AC

Printed in Singapore Set in 14 point Bernhard Modern Hand-lettering by Leah Palmer Preiss

Contents

NOV.
MODERN
MECHANIX
NOW
15¢
SEE PAGE 32
CENTS
LIVING
Thousands of Men
Wonders of this New
Drugless Gland

Bedtime

Five minutes, five minutes more, please!
  Let me stay five minutes more!
Can't I just finish the castle
  I'm building here on the floor?
Can't I just finish the story
  I'm reading here in my book?
Can't I just finish this bead-chain—
  It *almost* is finished, look!
Can't I just finish this game, please?
  When a game's once begun
It's a pity never to find out
  Whether you've lost or won.
Can't I just stay five minutes?
  Well, can't I stay just four?
Three minutes, then? two minutes?
  Can't I stay *one* minute more?

Eleanor Farjeon

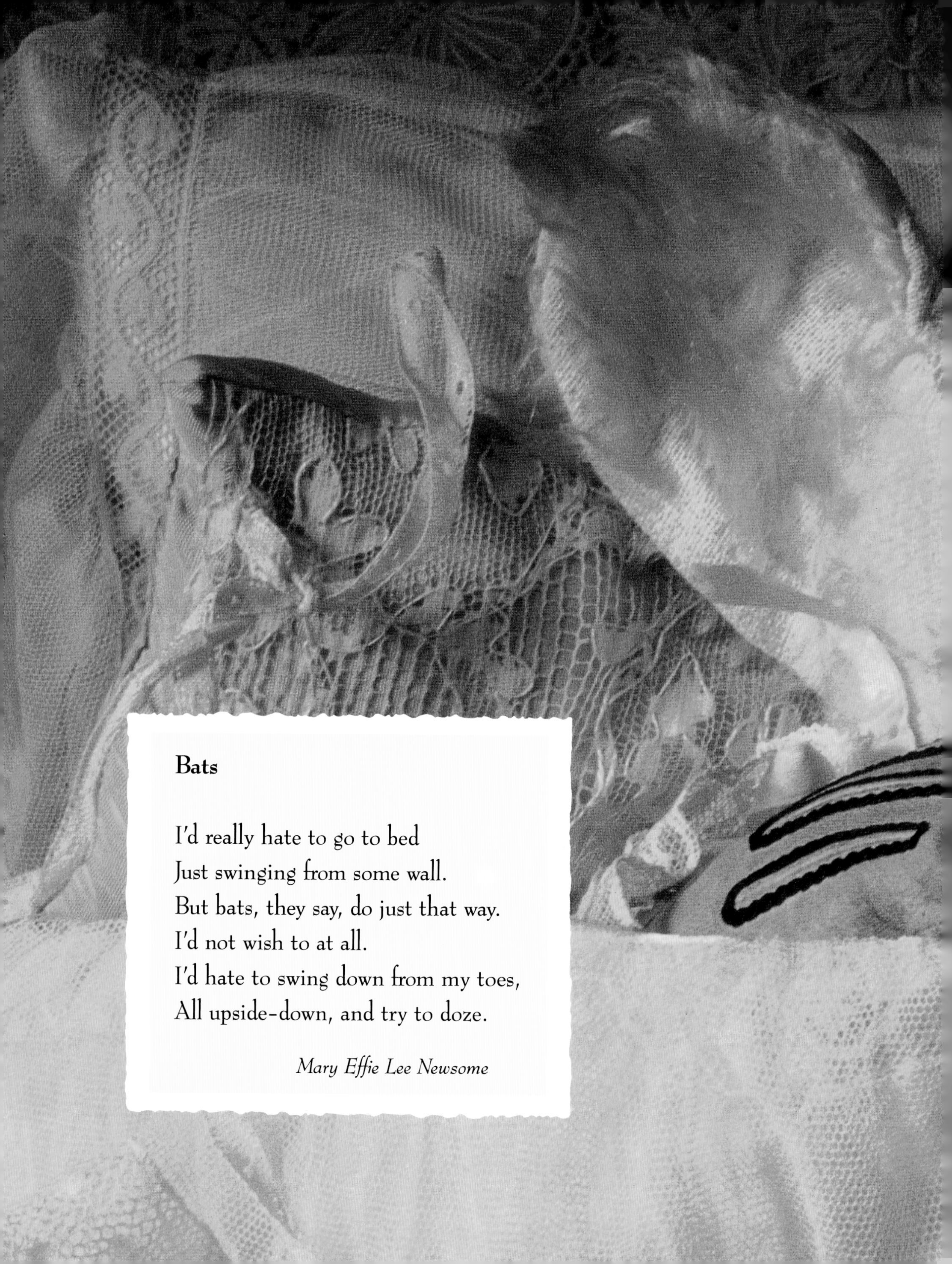

Bats

I'd really hate to go to bed
Just swinging from some wall.
But bats, they say, do just that way.
I'd not wish to at all.
I'd hate to swing down from my toes,
All upside-down, and try to doze.

Mary Effie Lee Newsome

Star Wish

Star light, star bright,
First star I see tonight,
I wish I may, I wish I might
Have the wish I wish tonight.

Traditional

The Man in the Moon

The Man in the Moon as he sails the sky
Is a very remarkable skipper.
But he made a mistake
When he tried to take
A drink of milk from the Dipper.

He dipped right into the Milky Way
And slowly and carefully filled it.
The Big Bear growled
And the Little Bear howled,
And scared him so he spilled it.

Anonymous

Sleeping Outdoors

Under the dark is a star,
Under the star is a tree,
Under the tree is a blanket,
And under the blanket is me.

Marchette Chute

The Night

The night
  creeps in
  around my head
  and snuggles down
  upon the bed,
  and makes lace pictures
  on the wall
  but doesn't say a word at all.

Myra Cohn Livingston

Escape at Bedtime

The lights from the parlor and kitchen shone out
   Through the blinds and the windows and bars;
And high overhead and all moving about,
   There were thousands of millions of stars.
There ne'er were such thousands of leaves on a tree,
   Nor of people in church or the Park,
As the crowds of the stars that looked down upon me,
   And that glittered and winked in the dark.
The Dog, and the Plough, and the Hunter, and all
   And the Star of the Sailor, and Mars,
These shone in the sky, and the pail by the wall
   Would be half full of water and stars.
They saw me at last, and they chased me with cries,
   And they soon had me packed into bed;
But the glory kept shining and bright in my eyes,
   And the stars going round in my head.

Robert Louis Stevenson

Sweet and Low

Sweet and low, sweet and low,
Wind of the western sea,
Low, low, breathe and blow,
Wind of the western sea!
Over the rolling waters go,
Come from the dying moon, and blow,
Blow him again to me;
While my little one, while my pretty one, sleeps.

Sleep and rest, sleep and rest,
Father will come to thee soon;
Rest, rest, on mother's breast,
Father will come to thee soon;
Father will come to his babe in the nest,
Silver sails all out of the west
Under the silver moon:
Sleep, my little one, sleep, my pretty one, sleep.

Alfred, Lord Tennyson

Gunpowder
This grade of tea brews into a delicate,
fragrant broth.
Imperial

Questions at Night

Why
Is the sky?

What starts the thunder overhead?
Who makes the crashing noise?
Are the angels falling out of bed?
Are they breaking all their toys?

Why does the sun go down so soon?
Why do the night-clouds crawl
Hungrily up to the new-laid moon
And swallow it, shell and all?

If there's a Bear among the stars,
As all the people say,
Won't he jump over those Pasture-bars
And drink up the Milky Way?

Does every star that happens to fall
Turn into a fire-fly?
Can't it ever get back to Heaven at all?
And why
Is the sky?

Louis Untermeyer

Sky Pictures

Sometimes a right white mountain
Or great soft polar bear,
Or lazy little flocks of sheep
Move on in the blue air.
The mountains tear themselves like floss,
The bears all melt away.
The little sheep will drift apart
In such a sudden way.
And then new sheep and mountains come.
New polar bears appear
And roll and tumble on again
Up in the skies so clear.
The polar bears would like to get
Where polar bears belong.
The mountains try too hard to stand
In one place firm and strong.
The little sheep all want to stop
And pasture in the sky,
But never can these things be done,
Although they try and try!

Mary Effie Lee Newsome

Wynken, Blynken, and Nod

Wynken, Blynken, and Nod one night
Sailed off in a wooden shoe—
Sailed on a river of crystal light
Into a sea of dew.
"Where are you going, and what do you wish?"
The old moon asked the three.
"We have come to fish for the herring-fish
That live in this beautiful sea;
Nets of silver and gold have we,"
Said Wynken,
Blynken,
And Nod.

The old moon laughed and sang a song,
As they rocked in the wooden shoe;
And the wind that sped them all night long
Ruffled the waves of dew;
The little stars were the herring-fish
That lived in the beautiful sea.
"Now cast your nets wherever you wish—
Never afeard we are!"
So cried the stars to the fishermen three,
Wynken,
Blynken,
And Nod.

All night long their nets they threw
To the stars in the twinkling foam—
Then down from the skies came the wooden shoe,
Bringing the fishermen home:
'Twas all so pretty a sail, it seemed
As if it could not be;
And some folk thought 'twas a dream they'd dreamed
Of sailing that beautiful sea;
But I shall name you the fishermen three:
Wynken,
Blynken,
And Nod.

Wynken and Blynken are two little eyes,
And Nod is a little head,
And the wooden shoe that sailed the skies
Is a wee one's trundle-bed;
So shut your eyes while Mother sings
Of wonderful sights that be,
And you shall see the beautiful things
As you rock on the misty sea
Where the old shoe rocked the fishermen three—
Wynken,
Blynken,
And Nod.

Eugene Field

Four Glimpses of Night
III.

Peddling
From door to door
Night sells
Black bags of peppermint stars
Heaping cones of vanilla moon
Until
His wares are gone
Then shuffles homeward
Jingling the gray coins
Of daybreak.

Frank Marshall Davis

The Night Will Never Stay

The night will never stay,
The night will still go by,
Though with a million stars
You pin it to the sky,
Though you bind it with the blowing wind
And buckle it with the moon,
The night will slip away
Like sorrow or a tune.

Eleanor Farjeon

MRS TITTLE-MOUSE
NUTKIN

The Land of Nod

From breakfast on through all the day
At home among my friends I stay;
But every night I go abroad
Afar into the land of Nod.

All by myself I have to go,
With none to tell me what to do—
All alone beside the streams
And up the mountainsides of dreams.

The strangest things are there for me,
Both things to eat and things to see,
And many frightening sights abroad
Till morning in the land of Nod.

Try as I like to find the way,
I never can get back by day,
Nor can remember plain and clear
The curious music that I hear.

Robert Louis Stevenson

Young Night Thought

All night long and every night,
When my mamma puts out the light,
I see the people marching by,
As plain as day, before my eye.

Armies and emperors and kings,
All carrying different kinds of things,
And marching in so grand a way,
You never saw the like by day.

So fine a show was never seen
At the great circus on the green:
For every kind of beast and man
Is marching in that caravan.

At first they move a little slow,
But still the faster on they go,
And still beside them close I keep
Until we reach the town of Sleep.

Robert Louis Stevenson

Pressman
1 TO 15
14

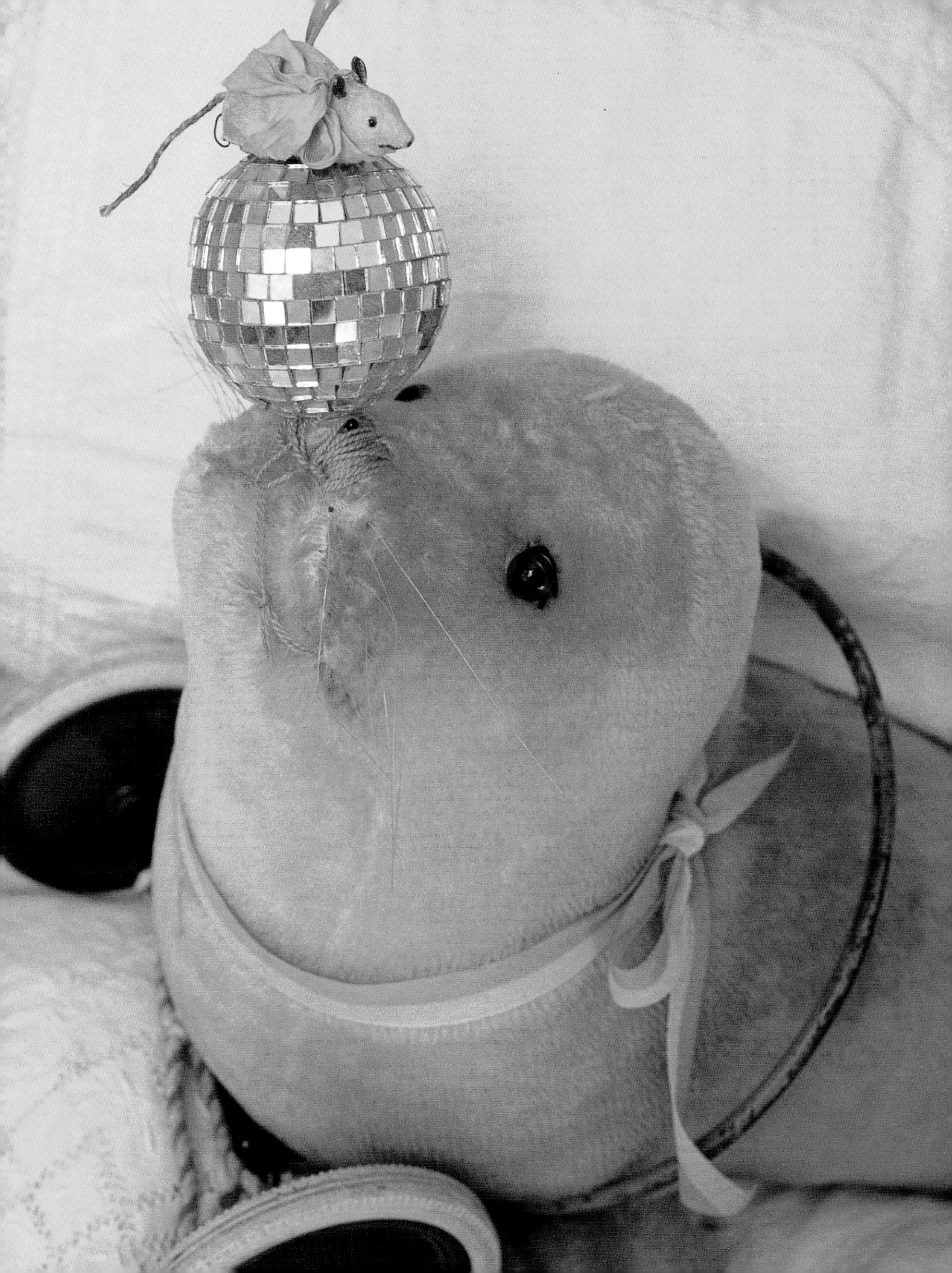

Seal Lullaby

Oh! hush thee, my baby, the night is behind us,
And black are the waters that sparkled so green.
The moon, o'er the combers, looks downward to find us
   At rest in the hollows that rustle between.
Where billow meets billow, there soft be thy pillow;
   Ah, weary wee flipperling, curl at thy ease!
The storm shall not wake thee, nor shark overtake thee,
   Asleep in the arms of the slow-swinging seas.

Rudyard Kipling

Tumbling

In jumping and tumbling
   We spend the whole day,
Till night by arriving
   Has finished our play.

What then? One and all,
   There's no more to be said,
As we tumbled all day,
   So we tumble to bed.

Anonymous

Good night, good night, now turn out the light,
Dream sweet dreams and travel safely through the night.

Michele Durkson Clise